STARTING OUT

MOTORCYCLES

MEG GREVE

CREATIVE EDUCATION • CREATIVE PAPERBACKS

CONT

ENTS

I SEE A MOTORCYCLE.

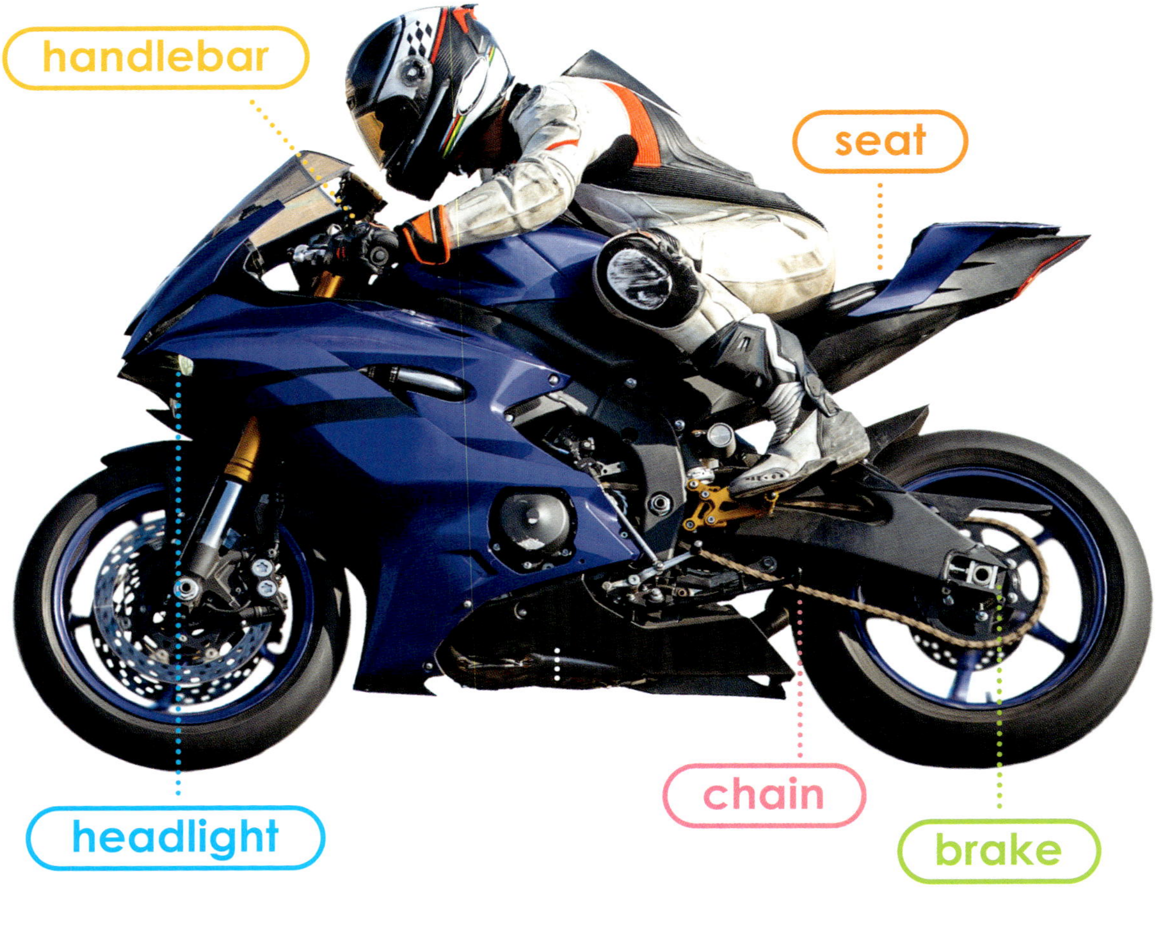

It is loud. It is fast.

Off it goes on two wheels!

Drivers balance. They use their hands and feet to make motorcycles go.

Drivers protect their heads with a helmet.

Dirt bikes are small motorcycles. Dirt bikes go offroad. They race around a track.

Motocross races are for dirt bikes.

burn

Pocket motorcycles can be as short as a baseball bat. Tower trikes can be as long as a giraffe.

Motorcycles of all sizes are fun to ride!

MAKE A NOISE

RRRUMM!

Can you make the sounds of a motorcycle?

Listen to these sounds:

https://www.youtube.com/watch?v=xhO89fhqnYo

Now it is your turn!

MOTORCYCLE WORDS

helmet: a hat that is made of strong material and that is worn to protect the head

motocross: a motorcycle race over rough terrain that includes hills, dirt, mud, and sharp turns

offroad: not on a street or road

track: a path to follow during a race

READING CORNER

Klepeis, Alicia Z. *Superfast Motorcycles*. Minneapolis, Minn: Pogo, 2021.

Slingerland, Janet. *Superfast Motorcycle Racing*. Minneapolis, Minn: Lerner, 2020.

Smith Jr., Charles R. *Bessie the Motorcycle Queen*. London: Orchard Books, 2022.

INDEX

PUBLISHED BY CREATIVE EDUCATION AND CREATIVE PAPERBACKS
P.O. Box 227, Mankato, Minnesota 56002
Creative Education and Creative Paperbacks are imprints of The Creative Company
www.thecreativecompany.us

LIBRARY OF CONGRESS CATALOGING-IN-PUBLICATION DATA
Names: Greve, Meg, author.
Title: Motorcycles / by Meg Greve.
Description: Mankato, Minnesota : Creative Education and Creative Paperbacks, [2025] | Series: Starting out | Includes bibliographical references and index. | Audience: Ages 4-7 | Audience: Grades K-1 | Summary: "Motorcycles will introduce budding book learners to a noisy, colorful world with this new Starting Out title. Colorful photos, labeled diagrams, 'Make a Noise' section, glossary, and more ignite a passion for learning"-- Provided by publisher.
Identifiers: LCCN 2023059471 (print) | LCCN 2023059472 (ebook) | ISBN 9798889891772 (library binding) | ISBN 9781682775622 (paperback) | ISBN 9798889891895 (ebook)
Subjects: LCSH: Motorcycles--Juvenile literature. | CYAC: Motorcycles. | LCGFT: Instructional and educational works.
Classification: LCC TL440.15 .G78 2025 (print) | LCC TL440.15 (ebook) | DDC 629.227/5--dc23/eng/20240129
LC record available at https://lccn.loc.gov/2023059471
LC ebook record available at https://lccn.loc.gov/2023059472

DESIGN AND PRODUCTION
Design by Rhea Magaro
Production by Beeline Media and Design
Art direction by Tom Morgan
Printed in the United States of America

PHOTOGRAPHS by Alamy (JoeFox Liverpool), Dreamstime (David San Segundo Navas), Getty Images (Mirco Lazzari), Shutterstock (Mr . Crocodile, Mikbiz, Oleksandr Lysenko, Idan Grunberg, Suradech Prapairat, Warren Price Photography, Bro Types, r.classen, Bohbeh, SKT Studio)